Top 10 Romance of 2012, 2015, and 2016,

> — BOOKLIST: THE NIGHT IS MINE, HOT
> POINT, HEART STRIKE

One of our favorite authors.

> — RT BOOK REVIEWS

Buchman has catapulted his way to the top tier of my favorite authors.

> — FRESH FICTION

A favorite author of mine. I'll read anything that carries his name, no questions asked. Meet your new favorite author!

> — THE SASSY BOOKSTER, FLASH OF
> FIRE

M.L. Buchman is guaranteed to get me lost in a good story.

> — THE READING CAFE, WAY OF THE
> WARRIOR: NSDQ

I love Buchman's writing. His vivid descriptions bring everything to life in an unforgettable way.

TWICE THE HEAT

AN OREGON FIREBIRDS ROMANCE

M. L. BUCHMAN

Buchman Bookworks

SIGN UP FOR M. L. BUCHMAN'S
NEWSLETTER TODAY

and receive:
Release News
Free Short Stories
a Free book

Do it today. Do it now.
http://free-book.mlbuchman.com

Other works by M. L. Buchman:

"*G*oing in."

"On your tail, bro," Amos followed close behind Drew's helicopter. "We're like stooping pigeons nailing those breadcrumbs."

"That's 'stooping hawks,' you dweeb. And those are fifteen hundred degree breadcrumbs." Drew carved an arc and dumped his load of water from the MD 520N's belly tank. Two hundred gallons sheeted down the front of the already burning house.

"But we're super brave pigeons." With most of the burning cedar doused for the moment—what doofus shingled with cedar and didn't keep the forest cut back from his house—Amos decided to dump his own fifteen hundred pounds of water across the burning trees that had ignited the front of the house in the first place.

"I'm a brave hawk anyway," Drew Shaw offered up one of his laughs on their private helo-to-helo frequency. "You, Berkowitz, just can't help following me along wherever I go, like the sad Brooklyn pigeon you are."

Now that was playing dirty. "Just making way for your monster Upper West Side ego, bro."

"Yes, some of us are just superior and know it."

Amos considered a couple of different response ploys, but none of them were going to pan out well. Drew was hard to knock down because he was a dashingly handsome black guy with a big smile and a clean-shaved scalp that shone in the sunlight or in the bars. Maybe he waxed it at night. Amos was always the frumpy Jewish sidekick with too much dark curly hair.

So, he let Drew have the round and focused on his flying.

Thankfully this house and the next had big swimming pools. Amos slid over his chosen pool and lowered the snorkel hose from his hovering helo. He hit the pump switch and sighted along the house's second-story deck to hold his altitude while he loaded up. His helo could suck up its own weight in water in under twenty seconds.

"Sure I follow you, Drew. Someone's got to clean up your poo." The FCC got pissy if you said "shit" over the radio—or even "pissy" for that matter. Really cramped a guy's style. What heli-aviation firefighter said "poo"?

It made the rebuttal doubly weak—both late and lame. Drew didn't even deign to answer. Instead, he just flashed one of those lady-killing smiles at him from where he hovered above the next pool over.

Twenty seconds later, Amos killed the pump switch, and lifted high enough to clear the house and return to its front yard. Sometimes they had to fly five or even ten minutes to find a water source. With those constrictions, the little MD 520Ns were of little use. Luckily this part of the wildfire was moving into a well-pooled neighborhood —bad for the neighborhood, but good for them. Saving houses was what the little helos of the Oregon Firebirds did best.

All six were aloft today, but the wildfire's front was such a mess that they'd split into three teams of two instead of their more typical two-of-three arrangement. These houses were on large plots of one and two acres, most with little attention to the wildland-urban interface they were creating. That meant that when a wildfire lit up the forest, it had a tendency to light up the houses as well.

The shared command frequency was quiet. After a long summer and most of fall, the Firebirds all knew their task sequence like it had been hardwired into their nervous system. Tank up. Douse each structure (burning or not) to soak it down. Don't fight the fire to a standstill—wasn't going to happen anyway at two hundred gallons at a time. Instead, cut a wedge and chase the fire around either side of the structure. Residents might not have to mow the lawn for a while, but they'd have a home to come back to.

As the day dragged on, their banter dragged as well. Which was fine. No point in using it all up before they hit the bar after the no-flying-past-sunset rule knocked them out of the sky. The boss had them on a two-beer limit— which was hard to hit because they also had an eight-hour, from-bottle-to-throttle limit and sunrise still came early. But banter and "I fly a firefighting helo for a living"— especially the latter—went a long way to loosening up the ladies for a night or three.

That he'd picked up Dad's workout habits didn't hurt either. Dad had learned the hard way that you couldn't support a family playing Division II soccer in the US. So he'd gotten into fashion photography, but never stopped with the workouts. They'd sweat together most nights in the basement gym. Mom had given up on him and left long before he became successful at fashion. He was successful in more ways then one. Drew had become used to finding hot women, models, randomly being there for breakfast, often wearing little more than one of Dad's shirts. Women liked a ripped guy. Something Amos had proved to himself well enough in high school.

That's how he'd gotten to know Drew—two New York boys both starting Army boot camp at the top of the fitness roster.

*J*ulie's silence was deeper than usual and it spoke volumes.

"Yeah," Natalie followed the direction of her twin's gaze.

No question, the Falcone sisters were in it deep this time. They'd been sent out to scout this front of the fire for their interagency hotshot crew. The fire northeast of Placerville, California was a late season burn and likely to be one of the last fires of the year, but that didn't make it any less ugly.

"Maybe…" Natalie nodded to the northern ridge.

The southern one had caught due to a wind shift not long after they'd crossed it—cutting them off from the rest of the crew. The main bulk of the fire was descending the rugged slopes from the east and would be here far too soon.

"Not so much," she answered her own thought. Even at a dead run, they'd be hard pushed to get clear over the north ridge before it too caught fire.

"Ouch," Julie could see the gathering smoke there as

well as she could.

"Out of the fire…"

"…into the fire."

They both turned west and stared. That was one of the problems with working with your twin, Julie saw the situation as clearly as Natalie herself did. The escarpment to the west was scalable, but it would take time. Dressed in double-layered Nomex and carrying twenty-five pounds of additional gear—not counting their fire axes, the chain saw, or the can of gas—meant it would take too long. Even shedding their gear might not be enough. And if they didn't clear it, the gear they were carrying was their only hope of survival.

Natalie pulled out her radio. "Hotshot patrol to Hotshot command. We're boxed in by fire in Grid 39-04, repeat three-niner-oh-four. Unless the winds change in the next ten minutes, we're going to have to shelter in place."

"Roger that. Julie, Natalie, you start prepping, I'll see if I can get some help."

She shared a look aloft with her sister.

"Smoke ceiling at three hundred and falling," she reported. "We're digging in."

There was a long pause before the acknowledgement came back. Three hundred feet was below where they could safely fly in a couple tankers of flame retardant. "Falling" meant that even the big helos would be shut out from entering this valley far too soon.

"Shelter in place" was the worst option there was on a wildfire. Actually second worst. It was one small, but important step up from being burned alive. She'd talked to survivors, and seen the ones who didn't—crisped despite their foil shelters.

They were past the need for words, not that they used them all that much with each other. With others, conversations always felt awkward and clunky by comparison. She and Julie simply knew.

Julie had a short-blade chainsaw and began clearing a circle. They were in a grove of arroyo willow and crackling-dry needlegrass. Better here than the bay laurel growing close downwind. Laurel burned hot—perhaps hot enough to melt a fire shelter.

While Julie wielded the saw, Natalie dug in with her Pulaski wildland axe. Hotshots worked in teams of twenty, forming long lines to quickly scrape an area down to mineral soil, clearing away all of the organics that could burn. She now had maybe ten minutes to do it by herself.

No shortcuts. She swung the adze of the Pulaski deep enough into the dirt to get below the needlegrass' root system and raked up a five inch-by-two foot swath. In the rhythm borne of a season's hard practice, she thought of an oval: keeping the tool in motion, cycling up, forward, down with minimal overlap on the prior cut, and another hard dig. She had an eight-by-two foot swatch cleared in under a minute. Returning the other way, she opened it up to eight-by-four feet. At six feet wide, there would be just enough room for them to lay their shelters side by side. Every two feet past that would be two more feet of safety from the fire. Fire that had leaped five hundred feet in three minutes to trap them here.

She didn't need to look up to know that Julie was dropping every tree that could fall on them so that they landed to the outside, as if the two of them were the center of an explosion. An explosion that hadn't happened yet, but would far too soon.

Natalie resisted looking up for as long as she could tolerate the unknown. When she couldn't stand it any longer, she sliced one more swath to prove she was stronger than the fear. It was a close call. Ten-by-sixteen feet clear of anything that would burn. But to all sides, she'd now mounded up a berm of dead grass and dead, fallen branches.

She looked at the sky first. The ceiling was down to a hundred feet. A tanker airplane needed at least a five hundred-foot ceiling for even marginal safety. No help coming.

Then she looked east. Minutes. At most. The fire was a living beast that had barely slowed as it crawled down the slope. Once it hit the flatland of the valley floor, it was going to race toward them.

"Two more trees," Julie called.

Natalie didn't even bother to respond. She raced around, busting up the berm of flammables though her arms were screaming with the sustained effort.

It didn't take much to stay motivated.

The fire's roar had become a distinct, basso rock-n-roll note.

That must be what the nineteen members of the Granite Mountain Hotshots who had been killed in the Yarnell burnover had heard. Killed—despite doing exactly the same steps she and Julie were doing. Dozens had survived burnovers with only minor scathing, but it was hard not to think about the Granite Mountain team—all killed at once, except for one lone scout who chance had placed in the clear. This time it was the two scouts who were in it.

Julie arrived in time to break the last berm with her and scatter it as far as they could.

Then they went to the middle of the scraped soil and chopped face holes. When the fire rolled over their shelters, the air would become superheated. By digging a foot-deep hole, they'd be able to breathe cooler air at the worst moments of the fire's passage.

"Now!" Julie cried out. She'd left the chainsaw and gas can back in the trees. They didn't need that exploding close beside them. They tossed their Pulaskis aside. If they so much as snagged the foil shelter on the tip of the axe, it would be a death knell.

They shook the thin shelters out carefully, turned so that the fire's wind ballooned them open. Their silvered coating caught the reds and golds of the nearing fire— almost pretty in the smoke-induced dusk.

"Dante would approve," Natalie wished she could erase the image from the sky the moment she said it.

"The seven circles of Hell brought to life," Julie concurred, reinforcing it in their brains.

Oh well. Natalie stepped in, placing her feet at one narrow end. She shrugged it up and over her helmet until all that showed was her front from calves to eyes—like the belly of a silver-backed caterpillar.

There was barely time for a last look around.

"Great idea for a change of pace, Julie."

"I've done better, Nat," Julie admitted.

They had been dating twins. The brothers had been handsome, self-assured, good lovers, and bastard cheating shitheads. The BCSs' non-twin brother had also been Julie and Natalie's boss, until the fiery breakup.

Let's have an adventure! Julie's suggestion had led them to trying out for and qualifying on a hotshot team. It had been way better than the clerical dead end they'd been stuck in. At least prior to this moment it had been better... still might be.

"See you on the other side. Love."

"Love. No more twins. Right?"

"Deal!" They said together.

And then they lay down side by side, placed their faces in the dug holes, and waited for the fire.

---

3

*I*t was late afternoon and the sandwich Amos had managed to cram down at noon was long since burned off. His gut was growling as loud as his helo's Rolls Royce turbine engine.

"Gotta get me a dinner bag on the next refuel, even if I have to eat from it like a horse." He told Drew—an idea which didn't sound all bad. Flying this close to fire took intense concentration and burned up the calories. It took both hands to fly an MD 520N to fire. Finding the third hand to hold a sandwich was tough.

They hovered low over a creek they'd found not far from a winery they were trying to save, loading up water as fast as they could.

"I'm thinking something to hold it, like a large wooden clip," Drew radioed back on their frequency. They always jumped a second radio away from the command frequency so that they could coordinate their own flight—which only had the two of them today.

"You got no imagination, bro. It should look like a

beautiful woman's hand, right down to the fingernail polish. Just holding it there, waiting for whenever you're ready for another bite." Water tank full, Amos kicked off the pumps and pulled aloft.

"Like there's a woman on the planet that would do that for a guy from Brooklyn." Drew took the lead toward the winery. They'd already saved the house and wine barn, it was the vineyard they were trying to save now.

"Way before an Upper Westie who—"

"This is Jana," the manager and part owner of the Oregon Firebirds cut in on the command frequency. "Report status by the numbers."

In seconds they'd run the list. Curt and Jasper were headed in for a refuel and food break. Stacy and Palo wouldn't be far behind them. He himself and Drew had enough fuel for another hour aloft.

"Drew and Amos. All haste. Two hotshots. Imminent burnover. Grid three-niner."

"Roger," Drew acknowledged for both of them.

Amos spun his helo to face southeast. The change in direction put him in the lead...and he wished it hadn't. Thirty-nine-oh-four was a blanket of smoke with fire on three sides and moving.

"We're in the Army now," Drew muttered.

They'd both flown OH-58D Kiowa scout helicopters in Iraq; not all that different from their present MD 520Ns. The Kiowas specialized in running low, down between the trees. Then, close to enemy lines, they'd pop up until their rotors were just level with the treetops to expose nothing except their mast-mounted sight—a multi-camera array the size of a beach ball that stuck up above the blades. A very low-profile machine. This was definitely going to be a down-in-the-trees mission. Except this time, rather than hiding in them to *avoid* enemy fire, the trees themselves were *on* fire.

He yanked up on the collective with his left hand and shoved the cyclic joystick forward with his right for maximum speed.

Unable to get any height because of the smoke ceiling, he veered left as they entered the grid area. Thirty-nine-oh-four was a kilometer-wide square between the burning hills, most of it covered with moderate-to-dense growth in the twenty- to forty-meter tall range.

About a third of it was already burning—flames leaping skyward, thick smoke in billows that looked like speeded-up film they were moving so fast. Trees literally exploding as their sap was superheated straight into steam.

Somewhere, in all that madness, they were looking for a pair of silver shelters the size of people.

Amos didn't have to look to know Drew would veer right. They'd run up the outside of the square, as close to the encroaching fire as they dared, box across the top, then down the middle before starting a square-pattern search. They'd done the move a hundred times in the Army and didn't need to talk about it.

Jana had given them the hotshot's radio frequency but he was getting no response.

"Got a feeling," he told Drew over the radio.

"Yeah, not a good one either."

Two reasons they wouldn't answer: they were in the fire already, or it was so close to them they couldn't hear the call over the roaring of the flames.

That was it!

"They're somewhere close by the firefront. Can't hear us."

Drew didn't answer. He'd be doing the same things Amos was.

Watching out for low smoke and tall trees.

Searching the terrain below for a flicker of silver foil shelter.

And nursing every single knot of speed he could out of his helicopter.

4

_____

*N*atalie lay with her face in the dirt.

"Don't come out, even when you think it's safe," she shouted at Julie. Julie already knew that, of course, but this was no time to rely on half-spoken twin-code.

"You don't either," Julie shouted back. Her voice was muffled by the two shelters.

They had their hands raised to either sides of their heads, hooked inside the foil to keep it pinned tight to the ground. The shelters were set close enough that they were in contact from elbow-to-wrist and boot-to-boot…and never had the distance felt greater. Foil shelters, heavy leather gloves, and the chasm of possibly imminent death.

"If you take one, please take both," she whispered to the fire gods. That was why they'd dated twins in the first place. As much as they drove each other crazy on occasion, she never wanted to live further than next door from her sister. Finding a way for men not to come between… *Yeah,* it had led to their current predicament—no matter how indirectly—but it didn't change the truth.

Something else not to leave to twin code. "I lov—"

The fire's roar, which had been building steadily, suddenly redoubled.

Quadrupled!

In training they'd told them that the fire-driven winds would batter at the shelter and she'd thought she'd be ready for that. Not even close.

The shelter's thin material hammered against her as if driving her into the dirt. It rippled and roared. The flapping was so fierce that it was hard to imagine that the material wouldn't shred, and harder still to keep it pinned to the ground.

Then there came the hammer blow!

So hard it almost hurt. It definitely knocked the wind out of her—and perhaps a scream with it.

Then…water came seeping in under the edge of the foil. In moments she went from lying on dirt to lying in mud. Her facehole filled with water until she had to raise her head to breathe.

"What the—"

"Unshelter now!" The command roared out at her.

She hesitated. It went against all training.

"Now!" It boomed over a PA system close enough to hurt her ears.

She took a deep breath, held it, and peeked. She was looking directly at a large metal bar hovering just inches from her face. Natalie had to blink twice to make sense of it…

It was a helicopter skid hovering inches over an area awash with water.

And close behind it was a tower of flame.

She didn't need to be told a third time. Not bothering to unshelter, she rose, grabbed the door handle and dove into the back of the small helo. She felt it lift, turn, and begin to move.

Only after she was in did her brain kick in.

"Julie!" The scream ripped out of her throat as she tried to wrestle the foil out of her face and see.

"Damn, lady. No need to shout, I can hear you." A man's voice. The pilot's? Didn't matter.

"Julie!" She shouted at him. "My sister!"

"My bro's got her," the pilot replied calmly.

Natalie finally managed to sit up and get the foil out of her face to look out the side window. A second helo flew close beside them. And there, still shrouded in silver, was Julie's face also plastered against the rear window.

She slapped the flat of her hand against the glass—and the door swung part way open.

"Shit!" She yanked it shut and latched it this time.

When Natalie looked out again, Julie waved. That was all that mattered.

"Any last words?" the pilot asked drily.

Natalie wondered what he was talking about. Then she looked between the two pilot seats out the windshield... and wished she hadn't. Apparently there was still more to care about. A lot more.

5

"*Well*, this looks like fun," Drew transmitted over the radio.

"What we live for," Amos did his best to keep it light.

They'd spotted the shelters in unison, too damn close to the center of the firefront. They probably should have bailed and let the sheltered hotshots take their chances. They'd made themselves a good hide. He and Drew should have dropped their water in a wedge between the fire and the shelters then gotten the hell out.

That was fire safety training.

But that wasn't Army training. "Leave no man behind" wasn't a motto, it was a way of life. The most elite rescue team of them all, the pararescue jumpers had the motto "That others may live." He and Drew had talked plenty about what *that* kind of commitment took. Talked about it enough that it too had become a part of them.

Now it looked as if that motto might come true.

They'd dumped their loads into the fire just above the shelters, then gone in to either side.

Thankfully, the hotshots had loaded fast, but it might

19

not be fast enough. The fire had circled. Both of the side burns were swinging in to close the gap. Any part of the valley not filled with fire was being obscured by smoke.

Going straight up would seem to make sense, but that way lay another kind of hurt. Even if the air controllers cleared the airspace of fast-moving tanker planes, traveling up into the smoke was bad news. It meant their air filters would be eating ash and all of them trying to breathe superheated air. Even filtered, it wasn't something he ever wanted to try.

"Fast and low, buddy," he called out.

"Fast and low," Drew answered back as they slalomed ahead.

Drew had the lead by ten feet, so Amos let him slide ahead. He tucked in one rotor diameter back and five feet up—just high enough that their rotors wouldn't intermesh in the case of a sudden move. Rather than watching ahead, he just watched Drew's helo. They'd perfected this back when dodging anti-aircraft—two helos flying like they were one.

Each tiny control maneuver that the lead pilot made, the tail pilot did the same. While the follow-position took immense concentration, it was concentration on only one thing: what the other pilot was doing. Rather than the dozen or more that Drew would be concentrating on. That left part of Amos' mind free for other tasks.

First, he called Jana with an update—enough of a one to get her attention, but not get fire safety after them if they survived this. There were some things that the upper echelons didn't need to know.

"Two hotshots heavy," Amos reported. "Coming out southwest corner. Kinda warm in this here valley. Figgered it was time ta be movin' along." No one on the team had a Texas accent except Jasper—and his wasn't much of one as his folks had moved to Oregon when he was six. Jasper didn't often speak anyway, though more now than before he'd hooked up with Jana—the lucky shit. If Amos lived through this, he was gonna find someone else that hot and maybe do some slowing down himself. Of course he and Drew had been saying that for a long time, but there was such a target-rich field to play in first that it was hard to care.

The "Texan" would alert Jana that when he said "kinda warm" it was way out of the norm.

One kilometer running flat out ahead of the firestorm was fast becoming the longest twenty-five seconds of his life.

Twenty.

Fifteen.

Now it was a pure race between the southern edge of the escarpment and the encroaching smoke and fire.

"Roger that. Y'all just keep your heads down and come home to Mama."

Amos wished he could spare a moment to stare down at the radio in surprise. Jana! Jana didn't speak Texan any more than the rest of them. Woman rarely joked at all.

"Who *are* you people?" The hotshot asked from the rear, but there wasn't time to answer. They'd been flying low—standard put-out-building-fire kind of low—which was far lower than running-like-your-tail-was-on-fire kind of low. Moving this close to the ground at this speed was something they'd only done once or twice in the Army.

Head down? So, not good.

Up ahead, Drew took them down another ten feet.

"Yipes!" The hotshot's exclamation was loud enough to hurt despite his headphones.

If he had time, he'd agree.

An instant later, the other four Firebirds raced straight

at them in two pairs—thirty feet higher, skimming just below the smoke ceiling, and only two rotors apart. They dumped their loads of water to either side of the escape path, knocking it wider for just a moment.

Amos raced after Drew as they hammered down the center of the momentary opening.

The other four helos would now be pulling max G's to make the turn. He wished he had a ground camera. All six Firebirds, flashing by in a long line just above the ground between two towering pillars of fire about to close. That was a moment to remember.

"By the numbers," Jana called—couldn't the woman at least *sound* worried?

Each of the six of them reported "clear" as they rolled clear from the fire front. It was hard to keep the adrenaline howl of laughter off the air. Sector 39-04 was now a hundred percent on fire, but they were clear.

"Damn that was close," the hotshot leaned forward between the two pilot seats.

Amos glanced over but any words died in his throat. He hadn't so much as seen her face when she dove aboard. Hadn't even connected that the hotshot was female until the second or third yell about her sister. Like the military, the hotshot teams were about twenty percent female and rising slowly. So, one in five that he'd rescue a female. One in twenty-five that they were both women.

He'd thought he was ready for all that. But his momentary glance aside from the path of Drew's flight had revealed her face. Still wearing full hotshot gear, she'd shed her foil shelter and her helmet. She had a long, elegant face framed in sleek brunette hair with light brown eyes that looked as if they were filled with triumph.

"Yeah," he managed, turning his attention back to the flight. "That was close."

6

"I swear to god, I had no idea she was a woman."

Amos laughed at his friend's expense plus a little extra to rub it in. They were halfway into dinner. Frank's Diner sat right on the edge of Finnon Lake just two miles from the Swansboro Country Airport where the Firebirds were stationed. The Placerville Airport was crammed with the bigger boys, so they'd been shoved off to the side. Thankfully, Frank's—the only restaurant for ten miles around—served up a fine feed and a cold beer.

"You sure?" Drew wasn't convinced yet.

"You blind, bro? Or was she that homely? Her sister… now that *was* hot."

"Never saw her face," Drew took a thoughtful bite of his double burger.

The guy still had such Upper West Side manners that he finished chewing before he continued the thought that Amos could see he was still in the middle of.

"Didn't speak once that I could hear. Was a little busy flying, you know. Not just trailing along like some baby robin following papa through the sky."

Amos was still hot on the trail of Drew not knowing he'd saved a woman, so he ignored the other dig.

Drew continued, "When we hit the ground, she—guess it could have been a she—said thanks and offered a solid handshake. Most of her face was blocked by the foil shelter she had all bundled up in her arms."

"'Cause she took one look at you, bro, and was afraid her face would melt. Using the shelter to fend you off, worse than fire."

"Just eat your damned chicken fried steak." Drew had never properly appreciated meat wrapped in too much deep-fried breading smothered in rich gravy. It was Amos' idea of heaven. His dad used to make it for him, when there weren't any fashion-model appetites around to appease.

Amos waved some of Frank's Garlicky Fries at Drew. "Telling you, the firefighter in my bird was flaming hot. And she yelled about the other one being her sister—musta been afraid you were gonna weasel out like usual and leave her behind. Can't imagine sisters falling that far apart in hotness."

"Remember the Claricks?"

Amos could only shudder. Drew had met one and set up a half-blind double date to include Amos and her sister. The first had seemed normal enough; the other definitely a coyote date—the kind you would gnaw your arm off to get away from what she passed off as a personality. Crazy town.

"I'm telling you though the one in my bird…freaking amazing."

"Get her name?"

Amos hadn't and was still kicking himself, but he wasn't going to admit it. "Got the name of the babe in yours…"

he teased. From her sister screaming it loud enough to knock his helo out of the sky.

"Julie," a voice said from over his right shoulder. "Julie Falcone."

Amos twisted around to see the woman who'd stepped out of the shadows behind their booth. It was the face from his helo. He'd never forget a face like that. And now it wasn't just framed by sweaty and muddy brunette hair, it was framed by a flowing miracle of shiny walnut brown that spilled down to her shoulders. Beautiful had become shocking. Her body, sweetly long and trim, was revealed by a tight red t-shirt from the mid-summer Dundee fire and tight jeans.

"No, Julie was your sister's name. You can't both be named Julie."

"Ha!" Drew laughed. "I knew you didn't get the name of the babe, er, woman in your helo."

"Hi," another Julie double stepped around from behind Julie. "I'm Natalie. I was the 'freaking amazing' one that was in the back of your helo."

He glanced at Drew, "You seeing double, bro?"

"Never been so happy to be," he mumbled softly. Then he jolted to his feet. "Would you ladies care to join us?"

Damn it! Drew's recovery time was incredible. Amos rose as well, but he was always a step slower than Drew on manners.

The twins—right down to the t-shirt and buff conditioning—exchanged a glance followed by an infinitesimal shared shrug.

"You saved our lives," Natalie answered for both of them. "That has to make up for your babe-this and hot-that. Some."

"Not all," Julie's look said she was less convinced, but resigned to her fate.

"Yeah, we're really…" Drew started.

"…sorry about that," Amos finished. "But getting to tease my bro about not even noticing he'd rescued a beautiful hotshot was too good a chance to miss."

"Your brother?" Natalie sat beside him, just close enough to smell like the outdoors and that delicious hint of fire smoke that could never be wholly scrubbed away. It was like ambrosia to a firefighter. On a woman as beautiful as Natalie, it was almost overwhelming.

"Well, other than him being from the snooty part of Manhattan…" Amos shrugged.

"…close enough to true," Drew admitted as he made room for Julie. "Though the good Lord knows I've tried to get rid of him."

"He says I'm like a bad Brooklyn rash. He's only jealous because he can't climb out of my shadow. Other than that, we're twins too." Despite his own pasty-white skin in contrast to Drew's clean-shaved dark coloring.

The women exchanged another one of those unreadable looks. Then Julie finally sat next to Drew. Her face ran to more serious expressions; Natalie's lighter nature had almost broken to a laugh. It made her eyes tip just a little more toward golden than her twin's.

7

"*Y*our solution to a bad breakup…" Amos looked at her in shock.

"…and losing their jobs…" Drew added in.

"And losing your jobs, was to become hotshots?"

Natalie answered with a nod as her mouth was presently full with a bite of her burger.

"What's next? First twin astronauts in space?"

"There's Mark and Scott Kelly," Julie pointed out.

"Not together," Drew noted.

Natalie liked that both guys simply assumed nothing was out of her and Julie's reach.

"Space…" Julie looked thoughtful.

Natalie worked hard to suppress a laugh. Julie was the master of the double entendre. Her dry tone also said space away from the two guys. They were clearly ladies' men, that had been obvious even without overhearing their earlier conversation. It was also clear that they rated Natalie and her sister as prime targets. And why shouldn't they? She and Julie were hot stuff, even if she did say so herself. Didn't mean she was going to sleep with one of them.

But she couldn't shake off that first look Amos had given her aboard the racing helicopter. Their survival had been in doubt, deep doubt based on the walls of flame visible out his front windshield. She'd been covered in mud and soot, and wearing full hotshot gear. And still, despite the crisis of the moment, he'd stared at her as if he'd seen a magazine centerfold. She and Julie were used to attention when they dressed up to hit a club and went dancing— they'd practiced as dance partners since they could walk and knew how to take over a floor. That wasn't how she'd looked after being dragged out of the fire.

Still, he looked at her that way.

And he and Drew were funny together, though it was clear that Amos was the punchline man of the team. Only rarely did he let Drew finish a sentence, but Drew's reactions also said that Amos rarely got his meaning wrong. It was a different kind of twin-speak than hers and Julie's, which she found intriguing.

"So, did you guys share a womb?"

"Considered it," Amos deadpanned it. "Drew's mom *is* awesome."

"She is," Drew agreed happily. "But imagine the trouble she'd have giving birth to this Jewish white boy from Brooklyn. He's such a whiner. Just didn't seem fair."

"Better than a hoity uptown piece of trash. He thinks he's smarter than me," he leaned forward to warn Julie. "Can you imagine?"

"I let him think he's smarter. His tiny ego needs all the help it can get." Drew made a point of looking to Julie to keep her included in the conversation.

Not many guys did that. Julie's quiet nature tended to let her fade into the background—which was fine with her sister. But both of these guys kept her involved, kept inviting her to stay engaged in small ways.

"Mrs. Berkowitz says that Amos was a real handful from birth to…"

"Until now! At least that's Mama's version," Amos laughed.

And Natalie found it easy to join in.

The meal slid by easily, very easily. Natalie found her guy-shield defenses lowering. Designed to rebuff the slavering toad, the grabby slime mold, and the inveterate ladies' man, it wasn't fending off the thoughtful guy who hid behind a mask of funny. Also, she'd seen them fly their helicopters like they were extensions of their very being. That didn't come from being a slacker in any way. The self-confidence they had in that area was hard won and fully deserved.

By the time they were leaving, she was idly wondering what other areas they were confident in—with reason. Things had shifted through the meal until there were two separate conversations. Julie and Drew talking about firefighting, spaceflight, and movies. Her own conversation with Amos was filled with enough laughter that her sides were pleasantly sore.

The guys drove an immaculate and testosterone-huge GMC Denali pickup. It had the Firebirds' logo on the door, red-and-orange flames on the hood, and was rigged for towing. It might be a company rig, but it fit them. The Falcone-mobile was a hard-used Subaru Forester wagon in mud-spattered bronze. It fit her and Julie.

"Is it named Carmine?" Amos looked down at their car.

Natalie laughed. That was usually the first joke out of anyone's mouth who heard their last name. Carmine Falcone—the villain of so many Batman tales—was usually placed as their father or brother. It was one of her tests actually. If a guy didn't get the joke, it was a big caution flag. If he overused it, it was another kind of flag.

Amos had struck a whole new balance by teasing her car.

"It is now." She glanced at Julie for her approval, but Julie wasn't there.

It took her a moment to spot her twin. She and Drew had walked well into the darkness away from the diner and were looking up at the stars together. An black arc was blocked out of the sky by the fire's smoke cloud to the north, but the main view over the quiet water of Finnon Lake was to the south where the rest of the sky glittered.

"Well, that's a first." Julie was very slow about warming up to guys. Sometimes she'd get in a mood, usually on the dance floor. Then her sister would burst out of her shell and shimmy like a sex goddess just to drive the men wild. It was one of the few moves that Natalie couldn't keep up with. But this wasn't that at all. They stood apart, but closer than was usual for Julie. Drew was darkly handsome and very smooth in his speech and manners—and it seemed to be working for him.

She turned back to realize that she was so close to Amos that she had to look up to see his eyes, barely lit by the neon "Open" sign in the diner's window. Amos had a cheery demeanor that seemed to see the bright side of everything. His rough edges, she realized, were a choice. Not an affectation, but a conscious choice of how he chose to approach the world: *here I am, deal with it.*

The neon sign winked out, plunging them deeper into darkness.

They stood little more than a breath apart. After an evening of chatter and laughter, his silence was echoing and pulled her in. Half a step was all it took. Half a step and they came together.

The comedian was gone. The rough edges gone as he leaned down the few inches to kiss her. Lightly as a question, deep as an answer. One hand on her waist, no longer sore with laughter but warm with anticipation. Another resting lightly on the small of her back forcing a sigh from her by its unexpected gentleness.

It would just be a kiss. She was a hotshot and would be back in the woods tomorrow. He'd be flying who knew where. There was only tonight.

But as the roughed-edged man smoothed out her own edges with such skill—another thing he deserved to be confident about—Natalie wished that there was a chance for more than this one moment.

8

"*D*oes it make me a bad man?" Amos asked Drew. He didn't do it over their shared frequency. He'd waited until they were back on the ground, getting fuel for their helos and food for their bellies.

"You mean that you hope this fire never gets a hundred percent contained?"

Amos sighed. It had started with that after-dinner kiss.

"Total bone melter."

"Had one of those myself," Drew agreed.

The next day they'd airlifted the twins out to reinsert with their hotshot team. The day after that, the Firebirds had offered transport to lift the entire team, heli-tack style, to a new section of the fire. Six helos could move three hotshots each. One flight had moved eighteen of the team. Then he and Drew had doubled back to pick up the twins and deliver them to a high ridge near their team from which to do some scouting before they rejoined the others.

They might have lingered for a few minutes. Truth be told, he'd wanted to shut down his helo and take the time then and there to discover just how good Natalie would feel if shed of her fire gear. Because she felt beyond amazing in it as she'd leaned into his kiss hard enough to pin him bonelessly against the door of the MD 520N. It had been a little weird to think of Drew and Julie doing the same not fifty feet away, but not too weird. He didn't know a better man than Drew—they'd both saved each other's lives so many times they'd stopped counting. Even guy-tallies hit their limit sometimes. And if Drew had gotten as good from Julie as he had from Natalie, more power to him.

Drew took another bite of his sandwich. "What are we gonna do about this, Amos?"

"Got me, bro. But we can't let this just slide away and fizzle out."

"Not this scale of heat."

They headed aloft no closer to a solution.

9

"*D*rew," Julie said as they took a thirty-second hydration break from cutting a new fireline.

"Amos," Natalie agreed before capping her bottle and reshouldering her Pulaski fire axe. Her muscles ached and zinged above the steady hum of pain that she'd come to identify with Day Four on a fire. She swallowed a couple of Tylenol with the last swirl of moisture in her mouth. In minutes, the smoke would make it achingly dry once again.

"Hotshots still?" she offered Julie when they shifted over to swamping branches—the arduous task of dragging clear the cuttings made by the sawyers. All of the burnable fuels had to be moved clear of the fireline and placed on the far side of the firebreak, which was thankfully downhill this time. Yesterday, it had to be cleared uphill over a hump. Absolute killer.

"One season enough?" Julie's thoughts echoed her own. It had been interesting, challenging, and hard work. The last didn't bother either of them, but after this one season the first two hadn't really grabbed them.

"Then what?"

That stopped them both long enough to stare at each other for a long thoughtful moment.

Julie glanced upward in a little double motion that said she wasn't merely looking at the overhead smoke.

Space.

They didn't have the degrees for that. Just like their mom and dad—who'd met on a building fire after coming from two different engine companies (as if that wasn't a slightly creepy echo of the current situation)—she and Julie had spent most of their lives in and around fires.

Space. While that might be out of their reach, they could do almost anything else. They'd long ago agreed that neither of them was interested in cashing in on their looks, though they'd had offers from the fashion runway to porn movies. But they were both smart and strong, especially after a season working as hotshots rather than Public Information Officer and inter-departmental liaison as they had back in their dumb-enough-to-date-twins days.

The firefight ran through that night and much of the next day, but they managed to halt the fire in its tracks. Helos and air tankers buzzed overhead. Air commanders above them. A second hotshot team did a set to the west and they held the line. Even the little Firebirds came in from their usual house-saving details to chase spot fires wherever they cropped up.

When the madness finally died down—over forty-eight after they'd arrived on side of the fire and started digging in for the fight—a dozer finally managed to cut a new road into the area. A Category II team rolled in with a trio of wildland fire engines to take over the cleanup. The hotshot team loaded up their gear—axes, saws, fuel, and their few scraps of camp gear—then began the long walk out. Not a one of them weren't stumbling like drunks. It had been two full days on the line with only a two-hour catnap.

Dropping off the adrenaline on the fireline left them with almost nothing to get out of these damned woods.

It was a pleasant surprise when less than a mile later, they broke out into the open.

"Pavement," Julie sighed happily.

"Civilization," another hotshot agreed. They stood along the edge of a one-lane road that felt like freedom.

"Cold water," Natalie could barely croak, but it would be near now. She had no idea exactly where they were; glad to just focus on lifting one foot after the next as someone else led them out of the woods.

The sun was setting, blood red in the smoke haze. It was a major improvement now that the fire was dying. They hadn't seen the sun since entering the diner for that first dinner with Drew and Amos.

Nobody was moving.

Maybe they'd just sleep here beside the road.

Then, by some miracle, a set of headlights stabbed through the descending darkness.

Not one, but two heaven-sent Denali pickups rolled up to stop in front of them.

"We heard your team was coming out this way," Amos grinned at her from the driver's seat. Drew sat beside him, his grin was even bigger. She didn't know if she'd ever been as happy to see anyone in her life. The cabins were full with other people, but she was more than happy to pile in the truck bed with the other hotshots.

Once they were loaded, the mood rose fast. Saved the final trudging walk, they'd beaten back the fire. She and Julie leaned shoulder to shoulder and enjoyed the others' laughter and joking. They'd not only beaten back another fire, they'd beaten back a fire *season*. The team would disband and scatter now through the winter months. Those who wanted to, would show up for the next season and bring on another set of rookies—just as she and Julie had been eight months ago.

But another season hotshotting wasn't for them. She didn't know what was, but that wasn't it.

The trucks were moving slowly up the narrow road. She smelled it first. The char—not of burning forest—but of cooking meat. Not burned past recognition—like the occasional deer or other wildlife who hadn't made good their escape from the fire. It smelled like...

"Food!" One of the crowd shouted out.

The trucks pulled into the driveway of a massive three-story house tucked back in the trees. Major bonus! The trees weren't burning.

Amos climbed down and was standing beside the truck bed. "Locals are so glad we all saved their homes, they're throwing us a party. Burgers and dogs on the grill. Hot showers and a swimming pool!" He had to shout the last over the cheers of the team.

Everyone scrambled and jumped down. When she and Julie reached the tail of the bed, Amos and Drew were waiting for them.

"You'll get dirty," she warned them as they reached out to help them down. Two days deep in the smoke, she and Julie were both darker than Drew—soot-black rather than beautiful brown.

"Caring about..."

"...this much." Both men held their thumb and forefinger pinched tightly together.

Her own gasp matched Julie's as they each were grabbed by their waist and set on the ground. Amos' enveloping hug was sweet, but his devouring kiss rang bells all up and down her body. When he finally let her go, she could see the full-body char outline she'd left on his clothes.

She pointed at it and he just shrugged happily before snugging her in against his side.

Drew rolled his eyes when he looked down at the matching imprint Julie had left on his own clothes. But he only sighed once before he shrugged and pulled Julie against his hip as well. Natalie had always loved walking arm-in-arm, though it had never been one of Julie's things. This time it didn't look as if she was minding it very much.

They showered, they ate, they belly flopped into the pool. The owners had a big hamper filled with men's swim trunks and various women's suits. After a quick glance consultation with Julie, they'd both selected the skimpiest bikinis they could find. Amos' and Drew's stunned-puppy reactions were well worth the hoots and catcalls from the rest of the team.

*J*ana waited and watched. She and her brother had founded the Oregon Firebirds eight months ago. They, along with Curt's best friend Jasper, had spent three years planning—and then gambled everything against this shot at launching a firefighting helicopter team.

It had turned out in ways she'd never imagined despite all of her careful planning.

The fires had burned and the jobs had flowed. They were still a year from being debt-free, maybe two—six helicopters and all of the personnel and support vehicles didn't come cheap. But they were far more cashflow positive than even her most optimistic projections. She'd built in contingencies and negotiated early payment bonuses as much as she could, and it had worked.

But it wasn't only the Oregon Firebirds that had exceeded expectations. The pilots and crew had come together not like fliers, but like family.

Her and Curt's biological family hadn't been much of a one. But the Oregon Firebirds...

Her brother and Stacy now frolicked in the deep end of the pool just like the newlyweds they were.

Palo watched raptly from the pool's edge as Maggie did a dive off the board that was as beautiful as she was.

And her own Jasper was easy to spot in his ever-present cowboy hat. He crossed the deck toward her carrying two fresh beers in one hand and a plate with a pair of enormous brownies in the other. He planted a kiss on the top of her head where she sat upright on a lounger.

He held her beer bottle steady until she had a good grasp on it with the hooks that had replaced her right hand and knocked her out of the sky into being an administrator rather than a pilot. He didn't see her having one arm as any bit of a handicap; he just helped in small, thoughtful ways.

"Good summer," he said softly, his voice tickling her ear as he slid into the lounger behind her and eased her back against his chest.

"Beyond good," she agreed and bit into the brownie. "I've been watching the boys."

Jasper's harrumph of irritation was a tease.

She knew that he knew what she meant.

"Look mighty happy, don't they?" Jasper waved his bottle toward them.

"They do." Drew and Amos were sporting with the twins in the pool. They were playing in a way that could only happen when it meant more than just the physical. There was a care there, an ease that she'd never have been able to see at the start of the season—not until Jasper had helped her discover it in herself.

"Might have heard this hotshot team was done for the season."

"Might have heard that myself," she agreed.

"Might have also heard that those two weren't real anxious to go hotshotting next year."

That she hadn't heard. She'd come to like Natalie and Julie, at least as much as she could in the few moments the boys had spared them for. Over burgers, potato salad, and massive bags of salty chips, they'd talked about past jobs— what they'd liked, what they hadn't.

"They're a fire family to the core."

"Daughters of a chief mother and a lieutenant father," Jana had gotten that from them as well.

"You got some ideas, pretty lady?" Jasper's hand slid around her waist to hold her close.

"Seems I might," his big hand spanned across her belly and made her feel so safe and sure. Sure of herself…and of them. "We've got that contract flying support for burn restoration. Could use some help with coordinating the effort. Field liaison and the like."

Jasper leaned down far enough to nuzzle a kiss against her temple. "That's my kind of Firebird."

And Jana knew that he was no longer talking about the twins. They'd talk more, but she just knew that between them they could make it fly. Drew and Julie. Amos and Natalie. The family would grow a little more and the Firebirds would fly a little higher.

But Jasper was talking about her.

Her wings had been cut when she'd lost her hand in that accident.

But as manager of the Firebirds, as a woman lying in the arms of the man who'd loved her since that first day when he was six and she was ten, she felt as if her wings had regrown. As long as she had these people around her —they could fly forever.

WILDFIRE AT DAWN
(EXCERPT)

IF YOU LIKED THIS, YOU'LL LOVE THE
SMOKEJUMPER NOVELS!

WILDFIRE AT DAWN

(EXCERPT)

*M*ount Hood Aviation's lead smokejumper Johnny Akbar Jepps rolled out of his lower bunk careful not to bang his head on the upper. Well, he tried to roll out, but every muscle fought him, making it more a crawl than a roll. He checked the clock on his phone. Late morning.

He'd slept twenty of the last twenty-four hours and his body felt as if he'd spent the entire time in one position. The coarse plank flooring had been worn smooth by thousands of feet hitting exactly this same spot year in and year out for decades. He managed to stand upright…then he felt it, his shoulders and legs screamed.

Oh, right.

The New Tillamook Burn. Just about the nastiest damn blaze he'd fought in a decade of jumping wildfires. Two hundred thousand acres—over three hundred square miles—of rugged Pacific Coast Range forest, poof! The worst forest fire in a decade for the Pacific Northwest, but they'd killed it off without a single fatality or losing a single town. There'd been a few bigger ones, out in the flatter

47

eastern part of Oregon state. But that much area—mostly on terrain too steep to climb even when it wasn't on fire—had been a horror.

Akbar opened the blackout curtain and winced against the summer brightness of blue sky and towering trees that lined the firefighter's camp. Tim was gone from the upper bunk, without kicking Akbar on his way out. He must have been as hazed out as Akbar felt.

He did a couple of side stretches and could feel every single minute of the eight straight days on the wildfire to contain the bastard, then the excruciating nine days more to convince it that it was dead enough to hand off to a Type II incident mop-up crew. Not since his beginning days on a hotshot crew had he spent seventeen days on a single fire.

And in all that time nothing more than catnaps in the acrid safety of the "black"—the burned-over section of a fire, black with char and stark with no hint of green foliage. The mop-up crews would be out there for weeks before it was dead past restarting, but at least it was truly done in. That fire wasn't merely contained; they'd killed it bad.

Yesterday morning, after demobilizing, his team of smokies had pitched into their bunks. No wonder he was so damned sore. His stretches worked out the worst of the kinks but he still must be looking like an old man stumbling about.

He looked down at the sheets. Damn it. They'd been fresh before he went to the fire, now he'd have to wash them again. He'd been too exhausted to shower before sleeping and they were all smeared with the dirt and soot that he could still feel caking his skin. Two-Tall Tim, his number two man and as tall as two of Akbar, kinda, wasn't in his bunk. His towel was missing from the hook.

Shower. Shower would be good. He grabbed his own

towel and headed down the dark, narrow hall to the far end of the bunk house. Every one of the dozen doors of his smoke teams were still closed, smokies still sacked out. A glance down another corridor and he could see that at least a couple of the Mount Hood Aviation helicopter crews were up, but most still had closed doors with no hint of light from open curtains sliding under them. All of MHA had gone above and beyond on this one.

"Hey, Tim." Sure enough, the tall Eurasian was in one of the shower stalls, propped up against the back wall letting the hot water stream over him.

"Akbar the Great lives," Two-Tall sounded half asleep.

"Mostly. Doghouse?" Akbar stripped down and hit the next stall. The old plywood dividers were flimsy with age and gray with too many showers. The Mount Hood Aviation firefighters' Hoodie One base camp had been a kids' summer camp for decades. Long since defunct, MHA had taken it over and converted the playfields into landing areas for their helicopters, and regraded the main road into a decent airstrip for the spotter and jump planes.

"Doghouse? Hell, yeah. I'm like ten thousand calories short." Two-Tall found some energy in his voice at the idea of a trip into town.

The Doghouse Inn was in the nearest town. Hood River lay about a half hour down the mountain and had exactly what they needed: smokejumper-sized portions and a very high ratio of awesomely fit young women come to windsurf the Columbia Gorge. The Gorge, which formed the Washington and Oregon border, provided a fantastically target-rich environment for a smokejumper too long in the woods.

"You're too tall to be short of anything," Akbar knew he was being a little slow to reply, but he'd only been awake for minutes.

"You're like a hundred thousand calories short of being even a halfway decent size," Tim was obviously recovering faster than he was.

"Just because my parents loved me instead of tying me to a rack every night ain't my problem, buddy."

He scrubbed and soaped and scrubbed some more until he felt mostly clean.

"I'm telling you, Two-Tall. Whoever invented the hot shower, that's the dude we should give the Nobel prize to."

"You say that every time."

"You arguing?"

He heard Tim give a satisfied groan as some muscle finally let go under the steamy hot water. "Not for a second."

Akbar stepped out and walked over to the line of sinks, smearing a hand back and forth to wipe the condensation from the sheet of stainless steel screwed to the wall. His hazy reflection still sported several smears of char.

"You so purdy, Akbar."

"Purdier than you, Two-Tall." He headed back into the shower to get the last of it.

"So not. You're jealous."

Akbar wasn't the least bit jealous. Yes, despite his lean height, Tim was handsome enough to sweep up any ladies he wanted.

But on his own, Akbar did pretty damn well himself. What he didn't have in height, he made up for with a proper smokejumper's muscled build. Mixed with his tan-dark Indian complexion, he did fine.

The real fun, of course, was when the two of them went cruising together. The women never knew what to make of the two of them side by side. The contrast kept them off balance enough to open even more doors.

He smiled as he toweled down. It also didn't hurt that

their opening answer to "what do you do" was "I jump out of planes to fight forest fires."

Worked every damn time. God he loved this job.

The small town of Hood River, a winding half-an-hour down the mountain from the MHA base camp, was hopping. Mid-June, colleges letting out. Students and the younger set of professors high-tailing it to the Gorge. They packed the bars and breweries and sidewalk cafes. Suddenly every other car on the street had a windsurfing board tied on the roof.

The snooty rich folks were up at the historic Timberline Lodge on Mount Hood itself, not far in the other direction from MHA. Down here it was a younger, thrill seeker set and you could feel the energy.

There were other restaurants in town that might have better pickings, but the Doghouse Inn was MHA tradition and it was a good luck charm—no smokie in his right mind messed with that. This was the bar where all of the MHA crew hung out. It didn't look like much from the outside, just a worn old brick building beaten by the Gorge's violent weather. Aged before its time, which had been long ago.

But inside was awesome. A long wooden bar stretched down one side with a half-jillion microbrew taps and a small but well-stocked kitchen at the far end. The dark wood paneling, even on the ceiling, was barely visible beneath thousands of pictures of doghouses sent from patrons all over the world. Miniature dachshunds in ornately decorated shoeboxes, massive Newfoundlands in backyard mansions that could easily house hundreds of their smaller kin, and everything in between. A gigantic

Snoopy atop his doghouse in full Red Baron fighting gear dominated the far wall. Rumor said Shulz himself had been here two owners before and drawn it.

Tables were grouped close together, some for standing and drinking, others for sitting and eating.

"Amy, sweetheart!" Two-Tall called out as they entered the bar. The perky redhead came out from behind the bar to receive a hug from Tim. Akbar got one in turn, so he wasn't complaining. Cute as could be and about his height; her hugs were better than taking most women to bed. Of course, Gerald the cook and the bar's co-owner was big enough and strong enough to squish either Tim or Akbar if they got even a tiny step out of line with his wife. Gerald was one amazingly lucky man.

Akbar grabbed a Walking Man stout and turned to assess the crowd. A couple of the air jocks were in. Carly and Steve were at a little table for two in the corner, obviously not interested in anyone's company but each others. Damn, that had happened fast. New guy on the base swept up one of the most beautiful women on the planet. One of these days he'd have to ask Steve how he'd done that. Or maybe not. It looked like they were settling in for the long haul; the big "M" was so not his own first choice.

Carly was also one of the best FBANs in the business. Akbar was a good Fire Behavior Analyst, had to be or he wouldn't have made it to first stick—lead smokie of the whole MHA crew. But Carly was something else again. He'd always found the Flame Witch, as she was often called, daunting and a bit scary besides; she knew the fire better than it did itself. Steve had latched on to one seriously driven lady. More power to him.

The selection of female tourists was especially good today, but no other smokies in yet. They'd be in soon enough…most of them had groaned awake and said they were coming as he and Two-Tall kicked their hallway doors, but not until they'd been on their way out—he and Tim had first pick. Actually some of the smokies were coming, others had told them quite succinctly where they could go—but hey, jumping into fiery hell is what they did for a living anyway, so no big change there.

A couple of the chopper pilots had nailed down a big table right in the middle of the bustling seating area: Jeannie, Mickey, and Vern. Good "field of fire" in the immediate area.

He and Tim headed over, but Akbar managed to snag the chair closest to the really hot lady with down-her-back curling dark-auburn hair at the next table over—set just right to see her profile easily. Hard shot, sitting there with her parents, but damn she was amazing. And if that was her mom, it said the woman would be good looking for a long time to come.

Two-Tall grimaced at him and Akbar offered him a comfortable "beat out your ass" grin. But this one didn't feel like that. Maybe it was the whole parental thing. He sat back and kept his mouth shut.

He made sure that Two-Tall could see his interest. That made Tim honor bound to try and cut Akbar out of the running.

LAURA JENSON HAD SPOTTED them coming into the restaurant. Her dad was only moments behind.

"Those two are walking like they just climbed off their first-ever horseback ride."

She had to laugh, they did. So stiff and awkward they barely managed to move upright. They didn't look like

first-time windsurfers, aching from the unexpected
workout. They'd also walked in like they thought they were
two gifts to god, which was even funnier. She turned away
to avoid laughing in their faces. Guys who thought like that
rarely appreciated getting a reality check.

Available at fine retailers everywhere.

ABOUT THE AUTHOR

M.L. Buchman started the first of, what is now over 50 novels and as many short stories, while flying from South Korea to ride his bicycle across the Australian Outback. Part of a solo around-the-world trip that ultimately launched his writing career.

All three of his military romantic suspense series—The Night Stalkers, Firehawks, and Delta Force—have had a title named "Top 10 Romance of the Year" by the American Library Association's *Booklist*. He also writes: contemporary romance, thrillers, and fantasy.

Past lives include: years as a project manager, rebuilding and single-handing a fifty-foot sailboat, both flying and jumping out of airplanes, and he has designed and built two houses. He is now making his living as a full-time writer on the Oregon Coast with his beloved wife and is constantly amazed at what you can do with a degree in Geophysics. You may keep up with his writing and receive a free book by subscribing to his newsletter at: www.mlbuchman.com

Join the conversation:
www.mlbuchman.com

Other works by M. L. Buchman:

Made in the USA
Columbia, SC
15 June 2018